BRAIN GAMES® kids

Awesome Activity Book

Phoenix International Publications, Inc.

Chicago • London • New York • Hamburg • Mexico City • Paris • Sydney

Illustrations: Robin Boyer, Karen Stormer Brooks, Peter Brosshauser, Mattia Cerato, Garry Colby, Mike Dammer, Dave Garbot, Dani Jones, Larry Jones, Kevin Kelly, Robbie Short, Jamie Smith, Chuck Whelon, K Kreto/Shutterstock.com (pattern on cover)

Brain Games is a registered trademark of Publications International, Ltd., and is used with permission.

Phoenix International Publications, Inc.
8501 West Higgins Road   59 Gloucester Place
Chicago, Illinois 60631   London W1U 8JJ

Permission is never granted for commercial purposes.

www.pikidsmedia.com

p i kids is a trademark of Phoenix International Publications, Inc., and is registered in the United States.

ISBN: 978-1-5037-4925-2

Manufactured in China.

8 7 6 5 4 3 2 1

LET THE PUZZLE FUN BEGIN!

Do you enjoy finding your way through a twisting and turning maze?

How about creating fun and wacky doodles?

And what about connecting numbered dots to reveal cool scenes?

With *Brain Games® Kids: Awesome Activity Book*, you can do all that—and more!

Every page of this book is like a brand-new adventure. One minute you're solving puzzles on a treasure hunt, the next you're searching for spooky words hidden in a scary word search. Sometimes there are multiple puzzles on a page, and sometimes there is just one large puzzle to tackle. No need to worry if you happen to get stuck; just turn to the back of the book and find the answer you need there.

Are you ready?
Turn the page and dive into your first puzzle adventure—the first of many!

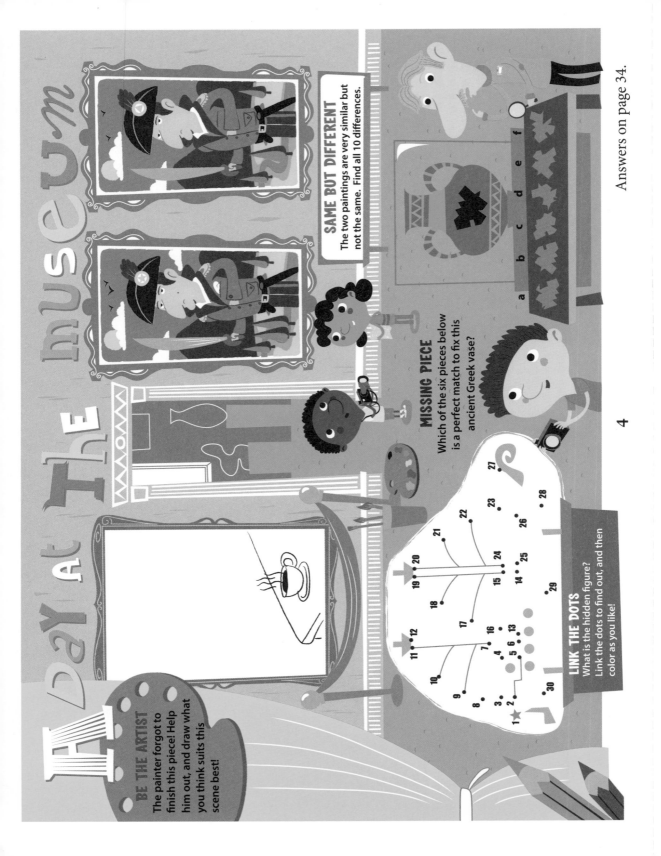

A Day At The museum

BE THE ARTIST
The painter forgot to finish this piece! Help him out, and draw what you think suits this scene best!

SAME BUT DIFFERENT
The two paintings are very similar but not the same. Find all 10 differences.

MISSING PIECE
Which of the six pieces below is a perfect match to fix this ancient Greek vase?

a b c d e f

LINK THE DOTS
What is the hidden figure? Link the dots to find out, and then color as you like!

Answers on page 34.

4

Answers on page 34.

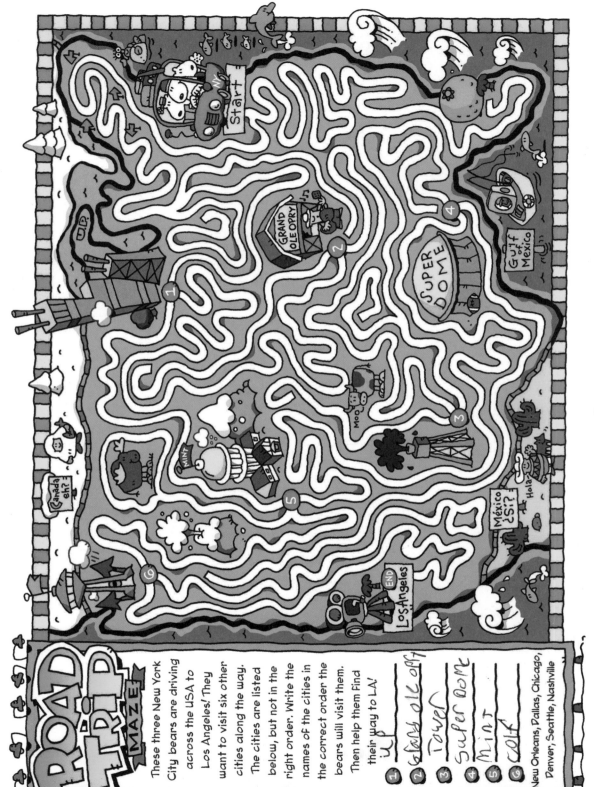

ROAD TRIP MAZE

These three New York City bears are driving across the USA to Los Angeles! They want to visit six other cities along the way. The cities are listed below, but not in the right order. Write the names of the cities in the correct order the bears will visit them. Then help them find their way to LA!

1 _____

2 Grand ole opry

3 Tower

4 Super Dome

5 Mint

6 Colf

New Orleans, Dallas, Chicago, Denver, Seattle, Nashville

SNOW DAY!

Find matching snowflakes around the page, then find the one-of-a-kind snowflake.

Starting at the arrow, follow the letters sideways, down, or diagonally to reveal a winter phrase.

L	E	B	O	A	V
U	R	S	I	P	E
K	H	N	O	P	W

BUILD A SNOWMAN!

Find the following objects in the scene below, then draw them on the snowman: two black eyes, three buttons, carrot, scarf, top hat, two stick arms, six circles for mouth.

Answers on page 34.

Answers on page 35.

9

Answers on page 35.

POLAR PLAYTIME

Answers on page 35.

Dive In!

FINISH THIS SCENE WITH YOUR FAVORITE SEA CREATURES AND OTHER UNDERWATER TREASURES.

12

Under the Sea

Find these objects in the **crusty coral**.

bubble
net
worm
hook
boat

Can you spot the five differences between these two sharks?

Help Gil the Guppy get home to his wife, Gillian.

START

FINISH

There are five pairs of matching fish. Can you spot them?

Answers on page 36.

13

SEA SURPRISE

Answers on page 36.

ON THE FARM

It's dinnertime!
Help Bessie back to the barn.

START

FINISH

Answers on page 36.

15

FUN IN THE PARK

Answers on page 36.

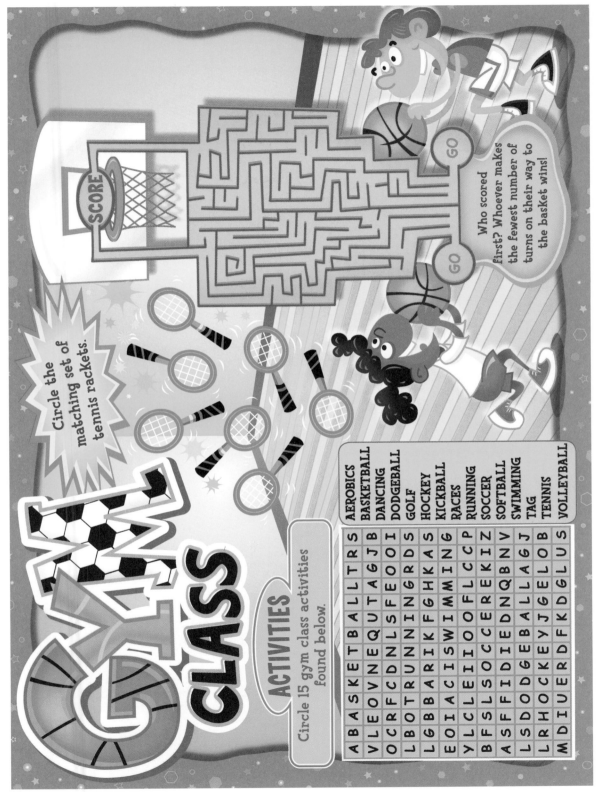

Answers on page 37.

PASTA-MANIA

Mamma Mia, that's a lot of spaghetti! Find your way from our hungry eater to the spicy meatball at the end!

YUM!

FINISH

Answers on page 37.

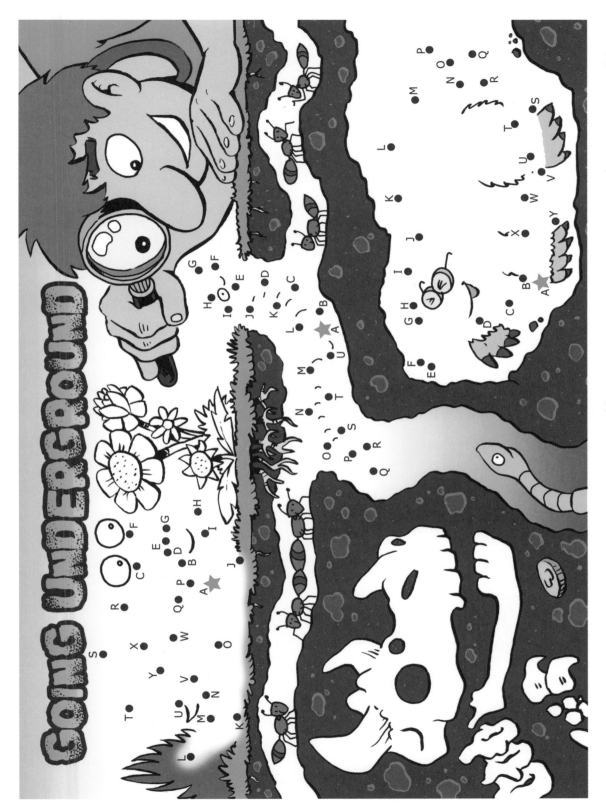

Answers on page 37.

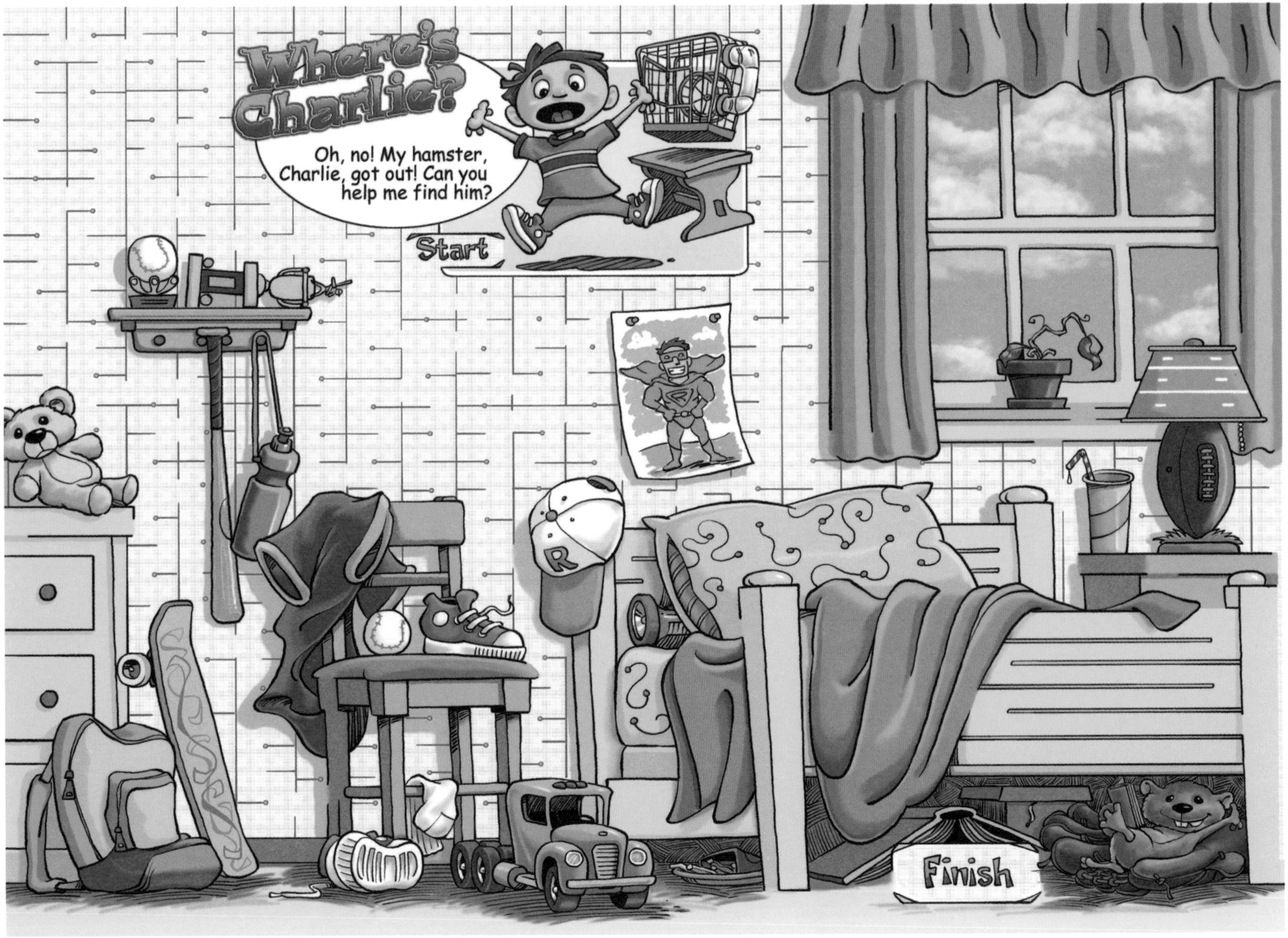

Answers on page 37.

TREASURE HUNT

Start your quest for ancient riches by jumping from skull to skull! Each skull must have even-numbered teeth and be touching each other. *Be Brave!*

START

Whew! You made it to the treasure trove. There are seven matching pairs of treasure chests. Find them, cross them out, and the one chest remaining is the one filled with treasure. *Yahoo!*

Answers on page 38.

SPLASHDOWN

Use letters from the word below to make as many new words as possible:

the water park

Follow the waterslides to find out which makes it to the end.

WORD SEARCH

Find the following words:

backstroke earplugs summer
cannonball goggles sunscreen
diving innertube swimsuit

```
N W V C E K O R T S K C A B T
Y U Z D Q Q U G U M T W Q D I
Z G H S B L U B O Q G H H I U
W W N O N A A O K G A H B V S
C A N N O N B A L L G G L I M
E B U T R E N N I G O L W N I
U S U N S C R E E N B Y E G W
E A R P L U G S R E M M U S S
```

TOWEL TIC-TAC-TOE

Play with a friend.

Answers on page 38.

Witch?! Way

HELP! THIS WITCH'S KITTY IS STUCK! CAN YOU HELP HER FIND THE WAY TO THE RESCUE?

KITTY

START

Can you find nine bats on this page?

FIND THESE SPOOKY WORDS!
(SIDEWAYS, UP, DOWN, BACKWARDS, AND DIAGONALLY)

J	G	Y	D	P	B	Z	P	K	G	R	E	U
W	A	E	I	S	E	M	G	H	O	S	T	N
E	U	R	O	L	I	A	M	T	U	J	C	H
N	F	I	W	E	R	E	W	O	L	F	E	B
N	Q	P	E	K	U	L	H	M	P	L	M	R
A	Y	M	U	M	W	D	N	I	L	B	O	F
I	F	R	A	N	K	E	N	S	T	E	I	N
A	M	V	D	T	C	E	L	A	Z	D	T	I
B	H	V	N	O	T	E	L	E	R	S	T	E
O	R	U	H	F	X	Z	O	M	B	I	E	C
B	A	T	L	O	G	N	W	V	H	R	Y	X
N	L	V	D	G	N	O	D	N	A	L	X	S

BAT, FRANKENSTEIN, GHOST, GOBLIN, HAUNTED HOUSE, MONSTER, MUMMY, SKELETON, VAMPIRE, WEREWOLF, ZOMBIE

Answers on page 38.

LIFE ON THE FARM

Castle Rescue

The princess is trapped in the castle tower! Help this noble knight find his way to rescue her, and then unscramble these words.

rgadno

_____

sltace

_____

snepisrc

_____

hitkng

_____

modgnik

_____

tamo

_____

drows

_____

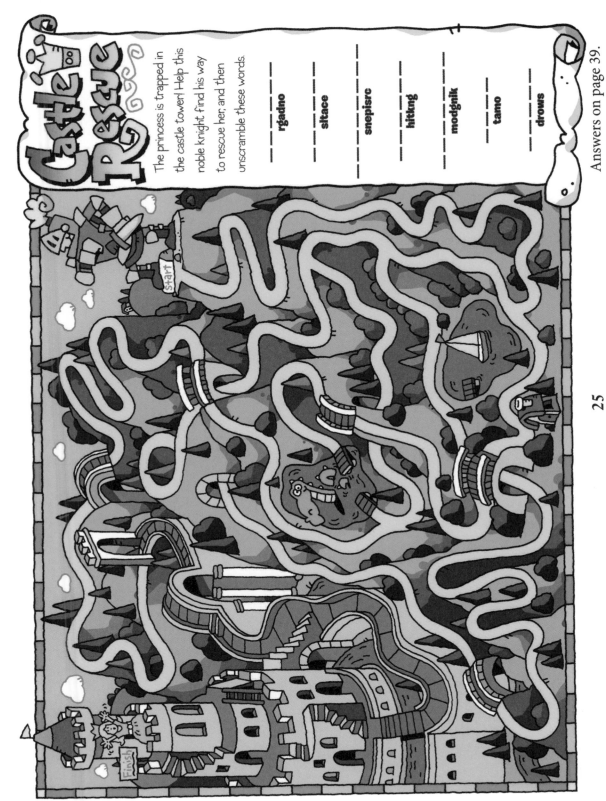

Start

Finish

Answers on page 39.

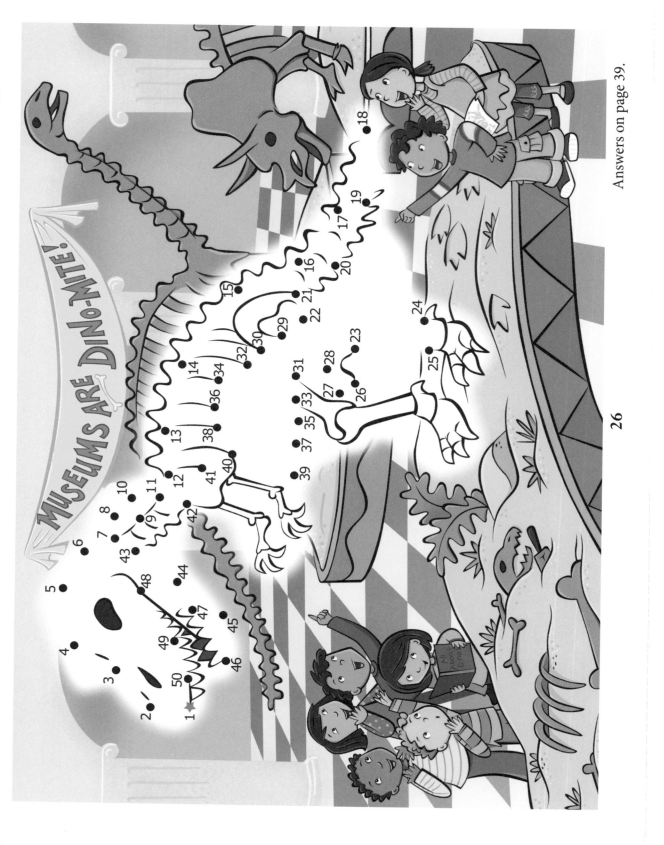

Answers on page 39.

Dinosaur Doodle

Draw this prehistoric pal in four easy steps. Give it other dinosaur friends, or create an entire Jurassic scene.

27

Answers on page 39.

Take A **WILD RIDE!**

Ride the Zoom-A-Loop all the way to the finish!

START

ZOOM·A·LOOP

Unscramble the safety rule for a free ride!

NAGH NO GITHT, SLPAEE!

ZOOM·A·LOOP

FINISH

Answers on page 39.

WORD SEARCH 9

BACKPACK, BOOKS, CALCULATOR, ERASER, LUNCH, NOTEBOOK, PAPER, PENCILS, RULER, SCISSORS

School Map

This new student needs to get to the cafeteria, but first he has to stop in the math, science, and history rooms in that order. Use the School Map to help him find his way!

Cafeteria — MILK — Science — History — English — P.E. — Math — 1st — Start — School Map

Monster Bash

Find all of the words in the list in the letters at the bottom.

GROSS-ERY LIST
broccoli
hairballs
newt
sardines
toadstool
toenails
warts

```
Y R I A X L E G N T N O
H S A R D I N E S D D M
M N H I Y H R E N Q R V
T M S G J A F P W A W R
B V N R K O P Q C T T P
Y X C U I T Q N B J R N
T L Y L O O T S D A O T
D E P S N G W F L A D E
T O E N A I L S X S D J
S Y I L O C C O R B O Y
S H A I R B A L L S A I
Z S T R A W G R Y T B T
```

MISSING PIECES
Look around the picture to find hidden objects: beetle, bone, bow tie, brain, flower, peppermint, snail, umbrella, worm

MONSTER MIRROR
Complete the picture above using the grid to draw a mirror image of the monster.

MONSTER MAZE
Use the maze to find your way from the monster's mouth to his stomach.

start here

finish

Answers on page 40.

Pumpkin Patch CHALLENGE

We found our pumpkins! Now help us get through the patch and the corn maze to the EXIT!

START

CORN MAZE

Oops

Sorry— GO BACK

Nope

EXIT

Answers on page 40.

Answers on page 40.

ANSWERS

A Day at the Museum (page 4)

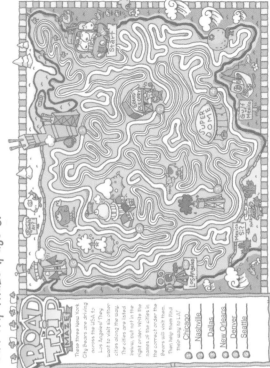

Road Trip Maze (page 6)

Monster Maker (page 5)

Snow Day! (page 7)

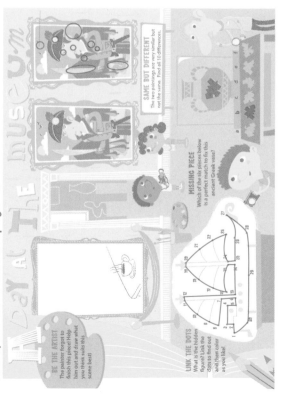

Day at the Beach (page 10)

Polar Playtime (page 11)

At the Pet Shop (page 8)

A Day at the Zoo (page 9)

On the Farm (page 15)

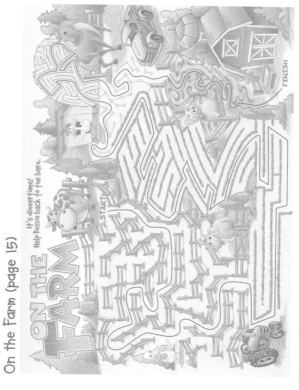

Under the Sea (page 13)

Fun in the Park (page 16)

Sea Surprise (page 14)

Going Underground (page 19)

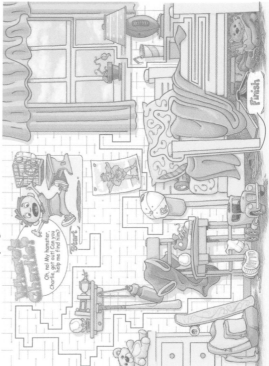

Where's Charlie? (page 20)

Gym Class (page 17)

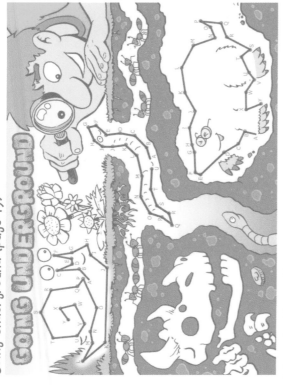

Pasta–Mania (page 18)

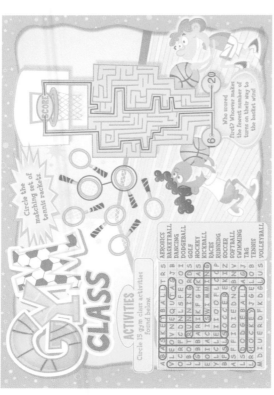

Witch Way?!! (page 23)

Treasure Hunt (page 21)

Life on the Farm (page 24)

The Water Park (page 22)

Rover's Lost! (page 28)

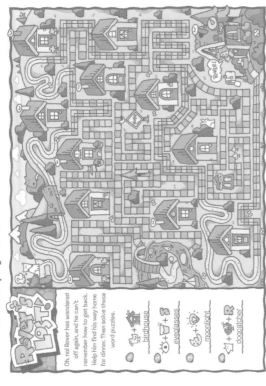

Oh, no! Rover has wandered off again, and he can't remember how to get back. Help him find his way home for dinner. Then solve these word puzzles.

🐕 + 🏠 = birdhouse

👁 + 🐝 + S = eyeglasses

🌙 + 💡 = moonlight

🐕 + 🎣 + R = dogcatcher

Take a Wild Ride! (page 29)

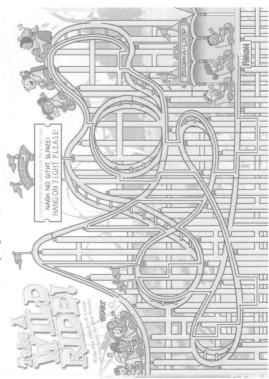

Unscramble the safety rule for a free ride!

NAGH NO GITHT, SLPAEE!
HANG ON TIGHT PLEASE!

Castle Rescue (page 25)

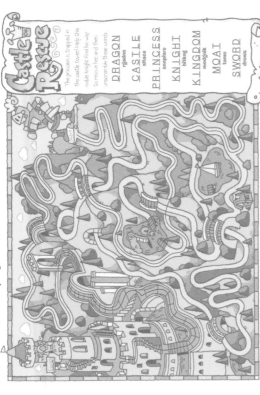

The princess is trapped in the castle tower! Help this noble knight find his way to rescue her and then unscramble these words.

DRAGON
ngrdao

CASTLE
etlasc

PRINCESS
sneipcsr

KNIGHT
kihtng

KINGDOM
mkodgin

MOAT
tamo

SWORD
drowss

Museums Are Dino-Mite! (page 26)

MUSEUMS ARE DINO-MITE!

Pumpkin Patch Challenge (page 32)

Jungle Exploration (page 33)

School Map (page 30)

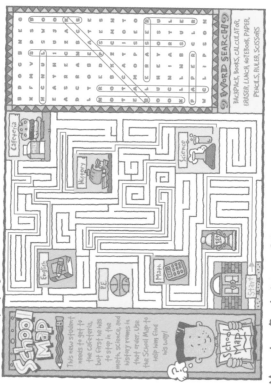

Monster Bash (page 31)